Queen
of the Universe

Written by Libby Gleeson
Illustrated by David Cox

An easy-to-read SOLO
for beginning readers

SOLOS

Southwood Books Limited
3 – 5 Islington High Street
London N1 9LQ

First published in Australia by Omnibus Books 1997

This edition published in the UK under licence from
Omnibus Books by
Southwood Books Limited, 2002.

Reprinted 2003

Text copyright © Libby Gleeson 1997
Illustrations copyright © David Cox 1997

Cover design by Lyn Mitchell

ISBN 1 903207 31 2

Printed in Hong Kong

A CIP catalogue record for this book is available
from the British Library

*For Jo and Jess, the actors in my family –
L.G.*

For Bridie – D.C.

Chapter 1

"I'm in the school play," said Gina,
at tea time.

She's four years older than me.

"That's nice," said Mum.
"Good on you," said Dad.

"I'm not in it," I said. But nobody heard.

"Squeak, squeak," said Mouse.
He's my little brother, and he's only
three. This week he's Mouse. Last
week he was Dog.

"I'm the star," said Gina. "Ms Hill made me the Queen of the Universe. I send my spaceships to the moon and the stars and the planets."

"I want to be a spaceman,"
I said. But nobody heard.

Mum looked at Gina. "OK, Queen
of the Universe, it's your turn to
clear the table."

Chapter 2

"I want to be in the school play too," I said to Mum. We were washing up.

"You're too young," she said.
"You can help me make Gina's
costume."

"I want to be in the school play too," I said to Dad. He was reading me a story.

"You're too young," he said. "You can help me make Gina's spaceship."

"I want to be in the school play too," I said to Gina, after the lights went out.

"You're too young," she said.
"You can help me learn my lines."
"I don't want to be too young," I
said. "I don't want to help anyone."

But I did.

Chapter 3

Mum got shiny silver paper and I helped cut out a crown for the Queen of the Universe.

Duck watched and said, "Quack, quack."

Dad got bits of wood and I helped hammer and nail a spaceship for the Queen of the Universe.

Cat watched and said, "Miaow, miaow."

Gina and I sat on the bedroom floor and she said her words for the play.

I listened.

I listened at breakfast.

I listened on the way to school.

I listened on the way home.

Soon I knew Gina's lines as well as she did.

Chapter 4

Every day, at lunchtime, I went to the hall.

Ms Hill walked up and down.

"No. No. *No*," she yelled at the
spacemen and their space dogs.
"That is not the way to come on
stage. Come from the other side."

She grinned at my sister. "Yes, Gina. You come on now. No, Ann. Come to the front of the stage."

Ms Hill got red in the face and put her hands over her eyes. *"Why* am I doing this?" she said.

A week before the show, a
spaceman tripped over his space
boots. He fell into the curtain at
the back of the stage. The curtain
dropped on everyone.

Ms Hill put her hands over her eyes. "Why *am* I doing this?" she said.

Three days before the show, a space dog called Chip (because it's chocolate all over) jumped off the stage and got its leg stuck in a can of white paint. It ran around and howled. It looked like a chocolate chip ice-cream.

The whole school came running.

Ms Hill put her hands over her eyes. "Why am I *doing* this?" she said.

Chapter 5

The day before the show, Gina woke up with spots on her face.

"Chickenpox," said Mum.

"Chickenpox," said Dad.

"Cheep cheep," said Bird.

"I can't have chickenpox," cried
Gina. "I'm the star." She put Mum's
make-up on over the spots.

"Wash your face and go to bed,"
said Mum. "No show for you."

Chapter 6

I took a note for Ms Hill. I waited for her to put her hands over her eyes and say, *"Why am I doing this?"*

She didn't.

She bit her lip. "The show must go on," she said. She sat down next to me.

"Have you been helping Gina learn her lines?"

"Yes."

"Do you know them all?"

"Yes."

"Can you say every word right now?"

"Ye–es." I knew what she wanted.

"No," I said. "No way. Not the Queen of the Universe. I'll be a spaceman, a space driver or a space dog. I'm too young. I'm too little."

"You will be the Queen of the Universe," said Ms Hill, "and you will do it well."

She grabbed my arm and dragged me to the hall.

She got Gina's costume and stuck pins in it everywhere.

She got a fluffy mop from the storeroom and dropped it on my head.

She got boxes to put inside the spaceship to make me taller.

And all the time she made me
say the lines, and I knew every one.

Chapter 7

So I did it.

Gina was in bed, all spotty, and I was on stage.

I wore her crown and I stood on a box to make me bigger and I said every line.

I sent my spaceships to the moon
and the stars and the planets.

I was the Queen of the Universe, and at the end of the play everyone clapped and cheered and stamped their feet.

Ms Hill clapped the loudest. She told everyone that Gina was sick. "But," she said, "her brother has saved the play."

Mum and Dad waved from the front row.

Everyone came backstage.

"Well done, son," said Dad.
"Great," said Mum.
"Croak," said Frog.

Libby Gleeson

I grew up in a family of six children and now I have three girls of my own. When I was little I told stories all the time. Now I write them down. There are always lots of stories in families.

Queen of the Universe began when I was thinking about the way little kids often follow older brothers and sisters around, admiring them, even though they seem to fight and argue all the time.

David Cox

I love drawing, and what I like most is to draw people in all kinds of moods and poses. When I am drawing someone who is angry, I make myself feel angry, or, if the person is happy, I smile and smile. In *Queen of the Universe* there are lots of different moods and lots of different movements. I had a good time doing these drawings.

More Solos!

Dog Star
Janeen Brian and Ann James

The Best Pet
Penny Matthews and Beth Norling

Fuzz the Famous Fly
Emily Rodda and Tom Jellett

Cat Chocolate
Kate Darling and Mitch Vane

Jade McKade
Jane Carroll and Virginia Barrett

I Want Earrings
Dyan Blacklock and Craig Smith

What a Mess Fang Fang
Sally Rippin

Cocky Colin
Richard Tulloch and Stephen Axelsen